Ducks Crossing

TREVOR WILSON

illustrated by Philip Webb

LEARNING
MEDIA®

Distributed in the United States of America by Pacific Learning,
P. O. Box 2723, Huntington Beach, CA 92647-0723
Website: www.pacificlearning.com

Published 1999 by Learning Media Limited,
Box 3293, Wellington 6001, New Zealand
Website: www.learningmedia.com

10 9 8 7 6 5 4

Printed in Hong Kong

ISBN 0 478 22904 6

PL 9008

Chapter 1

Sun City was way out west in a valley between high mountains. It was always bright with flowers because the sun was always shining.

Buck Handy was the mayor of Sun City. Mayor Handy was proud of his city. He was even prouder of its new, six-lane highway (called Handy Highway, of course). This was the only way in and out of Sun City. Every day it brought more and more people to live in that sunny place.

"More people, more votes," said Mayor Handy to his wife. "More votes mean that I'll be mayor for another four years, so I have to make sure that everyone knows who put in the super highway." And so he did. In every speech, he told the people what a good idea it had been to build the new highway.

But Handy Highway ran between two small lakes – Lake Grace and Moonlight Lake. People had been worried about that. They said that the highway would upset the birds that lived on the lakes.

Mayor Handy just said, "The birds can fly away and live somewhere else if they don't like it."

Chapter 2

So, all day and most of the night, the traffic roared along Handy Highway, in and out of Sun City. At first, the birds were scared, but they soon learned to live with the noise.

One day, a duck landed on Moonlight Lake. She had shiny, black feathers, with a white bar across each wing. Her real home was on Lake Grace, but she'd been chased away from it by a mean old drake.

When she had settled her ruffled
feathers, she looked for a spot to build a
nest. She found a good place in a clump
of reeds. There she laid six eggs.

The duck sat on her eggs and kept them
warm. Day after day she sat there,
making little noises to herself.

At last she felt something
happening to the eggs,
and in no time at all,
she had six fluffy
ducklings.

Now that she was a mother, the duck was very busy. She showed her ducklings how to swim and made sure that they kept close to her at all times.

But she didn't care much for Moonlight Lake. She decided to go back to her real home on Lake Grace. So, one day, with her six fluffy ducklings cheeping behind her, she climbed up the bank.

At the edge of Handy Highway, she
looked around to see that they were all
there.

"Cheep, cheep," went the ducklings,
and off they all waddled.

Chapter 3

Just as the mother duck started to cross Handy Highway, a car went speeding by. The mother duck jumped back and fell over her ducklings. Each time she tried to cross, the same thing happened. Every driver was in a hurry to get someplace fast.

An old man in a rattletrap truck saw
what was happening. He pulled off the
highway into a rest stop. He got out and
walked over to the mother duck. He
shook his head.

"There's no way you'll get across here,
Mother Ducky," he said.

"Quack!" went the mother duck.

"Cheep, cheep," went the ducklings.

Another car pulled up. A mother and her daughter climbed out. "Look at the little ducklings!" cried the little girl. "They're so cute."

"They want to cross the highway," said her mother.

"They'll never make it," said the old man.

More cars pulled off the highway till there was no more room in the rest stop. Soon, quite a crowd had gathered. "Stop the traffic," they called. "Let the ducks cross the road."

"Anyone who tries to stop this traffic had better be careful," said the old man. "We could have a bad accident here."

"Quack!" went the mother duck.

"Cheep, cheep," went the ducklings.

"I've got a cell phone," said the little girl's mother. "I'll call the chief of police."

The chief of police answered his phone. "What!" he said. "Stop the traffic on Handy Highway? Forget it! This is the busiest time of the day."

"If something isn't done," said the little girl's mother, "there's going to be an accident."

"What's the trouble?" asked the chief of police.

"A mother duck wants to cross the road," she said.

Chapter 4

The chief of police was a big man. He liked his uniform with its bright silver buttons. He drove out onto Handy Highway with every light on his car flashing. He even turned on the siren to show how important he was.

When he reached the rest stop, he climbed out of his car, puffed out his chest, and stomped over to the crowd. "Now, what's all this about?" he yelled.

"Quack!" went the mother duck, trying to cross the road again.

"Careful, careful!" said the old man.

"Please save the ducklings!" cried the little girl.

"Stop the traffic!" shouted the crowd.

"No way!" yelled the chief.

But the chief could see that the people were getting angry. He didn't know what to do. So he called the mayor.

Mayor Handy was speaking to some very important visitors from out of town. They wanted to build a huge hotel next to the two lakes. Mayor Handy thought that this was a great idea. "More people, more money, and more votes," he thought.

Chapter 5

Suddenly the mayor's secretary, Miss Pink, hurried in and whispered to him. The mayor spluttered, and his eyebrows went up and down. He turned back to his visitors.

"Something urgent has come up out by Lake Grace," he said. "Would you like to look round city hall? I should be back soon."

"No, we'll come too," said the visitors. "That's where we want to build the new hotel."

When Mayor Handy and his guests drove up, there was just enough room to park. He looked very annoyed as he climbed out of the car. "What's going on here?" he demanded.

"These ducks want to cross the road," said the old man.

"Stop the traffic!" shouted the crowd.

"No way!" yelled the chief of police.

"Quack!" went the mother duck.

"Cheep, cheep," went the ducklings.

A television crew was driving past. They saw the crowd, and their van screeched to a stop.

"Get this on film," said the reporter. "This will be a good story for the evening news." He ran over to the crowd. "What's the trouble?" he asked the old man.

"The ducks want to cross the road," said the old man.

"Stop the traffic!" shouted the crowd.

"No way!" yelled the chief of police.

Suddenly, one of the mayor's visitors said, "We can't build our hotel here. That's a rare white-wing duck. If it gets hurt, there'll be big trouble."

Mayor Handy was thinking fast. "This could be worth a lot of votes. If I don't do the right thing, they will be votes against me."

"All we have to do is get this duck and her ducklings across the highway," said the old man.

"But they might be killed!" cried the little girl.

"Stop the traffic!" shouted the crowd.

"No way!" yelled the chief of police.

Just then, the mother duck tried once more to cross the highway. A car almost hit her.

The duck jumped back, quacking loudly. The six fluffy, yellow ducklings crowded round her, cheeping in alarm.

"Well, now," said Mayor Handy. He puffed out his chest and looked into the television camera. "We have a duty to look after our wildlife," he said.

Chapter 6

"You'd better hurry, Mayor Handy," said the television reporter. "That duck is not going to give up."

"Stop the traffic!" shouted the crowd.

"No way!" yelled the chief of police.

"Well, Mr. Mayor?" said the television reporter.

"Stop the traffic," said the mayor. He turned to the chief of police. "Get out there and stop the traffic."

The chief went red in the face. "Mr. Mayor, sir, there's no way ..."

"Just look at that," laughed the old man. "The traffic is stopping by itself."

"So it is," said the visitors. "The cars are slowing down to see what all the fuss is about."

As the cars rolled to a stop, the chief of police stepped out and held up his hand. "Stop!" he yelled as loud as he could.

He kept walking until he was in the middle of the six lanes. Standing there with the television camera on him, he felt more important than he'd ever felt before. He waved to the mother duck. "Come on, come on!" he called.

"Just a moment," said the mayor. He wanted everyone to look at him. "Let me do this."

Proudly, Mayor Handy led the mother duck and her six fluffy ducklings across the highway. The chief of police followed him, still holding up his hand and trying to look important.

"Bye, Mother Ducky!" called the old man.

"Well done!" cheered the crowd.

"I loved those little ducklings," said the little girl.

When the ducks reached the other side of Handy Highway, the drivers remembered that they were in a hurry. The traffic started up again with a roar. The television crew packed up their gear and hurried to the station to catch the evening news.

"All's well that ends well," said the old man, getting back into his rattletrap truck.

But across the highway, the mayor glared at the chief of police. "You fool," he said. "Why did you let the traffic start again? Now we're stuck on this side of the highway. How are we going to get back? You'll have to stop the traffic again."

"No way," said the chief of police.

"Quack!" went the mother duck, gliding out onto Lake Grace.

"Cheep, cheep," went the ducklings, paddling their little legs to keep up with her.